THE
CASE OF THE INVISIBLE CAT

Look for these books in the
Clue™ series:

THE
CASE OF THE INVISIBLE CAT

Book created by A. E. Parker

Written by Eric Weiner

Based on characters from the Parker Brothers game

A Creative Media Applications Production

SCHOLASTIC INC.
New York Toronto London Auckland Sydney

*Special thanks to: Thomas Dusenberry,
Julie Ryan, Laura Millhollin, Jean Feiwel,
Greg Holch, Dona Smith, Nancy Smith,
John Simko, and Elizabeth Parisi.*

ISBN 0-590-45632-6

Copyright © 1992 by Waddingtons Games Ltd. All rights reserved. Published by Scholastic Inc., by arrangement with Parker Bros., a division of Tonka Corp., 1027 Newport Avenue, Pawtucket, RI 02862. CLUE® is a registered trademark of Waddingtons Games Ltd. for its detective games equipment.

12 11 10 9 8 7 6 5 4   3 4 5 6 7/9

Printed in the U.S.A.   40

First Scholastic printing, December 1992

For Matthew and Andrew

Contents

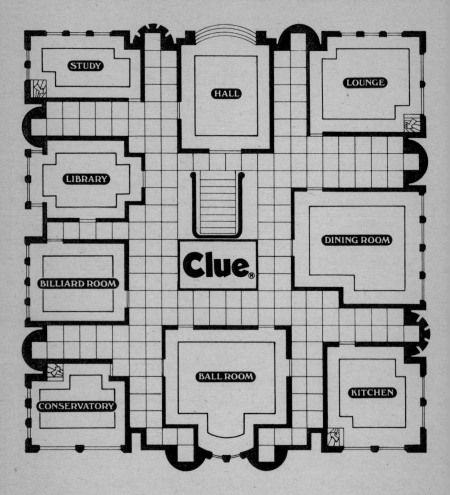

Allow Me to Introduce Myself . . .

MY NAME IS REGINALD BODDY, AND I'M your host for the weekend. Please give your bags — and your weapons — to my maid, Mrs. White. I have no intention of being murdered again.

Hmm . . . I should probably explain about that. It seems that during your previous visit one of the other guests accidentally shot at me. Three times.

Everyone thought I was hit, but as it happens, I had just swallowed some snake venom antidote. That was what knocked me cold. Never mind, I'm fit as a fiddle now!

Well, enough about that! The important thing is that you're here and that this time there won't be any ghastly crimes. Not a single one. I promise you.

But . . . just in case there *is* a crime . . .

Would you mind keeping a lookout? Watch for clues. That sort of thing. Then tell me who committed each crime. Okeydoke?

You have only six suspects to worry about. (I,

1

of course, will never be a suspect!) The six suspects are:

Colonel Mustard: A dashing gallant who's always ready to fight a duel. In fact, I often find that when I'm around the Colonel, I'm dashing, too. Dashing the other way!

Mrs. Peacock: What can one say about this prim and proper lady? Whatever it is, you'd better mind your manners!

Miss Scarlet: What a stunning woman. (At least, it was stunning when she hit me with the Lead Pipe.)

Professor Plum: Once you meet the Professor, you'll never forget him. On the other hand, he never remembers a thing!

Mrs. White: My maid is always cheerful, always wearing a smile. Why, she just loves being in the Kitchen, sharpening the Knives.

Mr. Green: All right, so this businessman is a bit of a bully. There are worse things he could be. (And he's been all of them.)

Don't worry. I'll give you a chart of the suspects, weapons, and rooms at the end of each mystery. As you read, you can check off the suspects until you've narrowed your list down to one.

But as I say, all of this will be totally unnecessary because this time there isn't going to be any trouble and there won't be any screams coming from the Hall.

Er, did I just hear screams coming from the Hall?

Excuse me a moment, would you?

1.
A Mixed Bag

THERE WAS A LOUD KNOCK ON THE front door of Mr. Boddy's mansion. Mrs. White, the maid, hurried to open it.

Before her stood a tall, dashing gentleman in a yellow cap, yellow coat, and yellow boots. "Colonel Mustard," said Mrs. White with a broad smile. "It's always a pleasure to see you!"

As the Colonel strode past her, Mrs. White's smile changed to a snarl. "It would be an even greater pleasure *not* to see you," she muttered under her breath.

"Let me take your bag," she said aloud, reaching for the Colonel's black leather suitcase.

But her hand never reached it.

Mustard whipped out a Revolver and fired three times.

Mr. Boddy raced in. He found the Colonel with his Revolver raised high in the air. His monocle was quivering. So was Mrs. White.

"Those were just warning shots," explained the Colonel. "But let this be a lesson to you — and to anyone else who tries to touch my suitcase this weekend. This bag is filled with priceless statues that I collected abroad, while serving in the army. I'm meeting a buyer here on Sunday and I don't intend to lose my fortune to a thief." He glared at Mrs. White.

"Thief?" echoed Mrs. White, shocked.

"Calling me a thief?" shouted the Colonel, waving his Revolver. "I challenge you to a duel!"

"Hold on, Mustard. You called *her* a thief," explained a worried-looking Mr. Boddy.

"Did I? Ah. Well, in that case." Mustard put away the Revolver and headed for his room, clutching his suitcase with both hands.

Just then, there was another knock at the door. Mrs. White opened it. Outside, there stood a beautiful woman in a dark red coat with bright red rouge on her cheeks.

"Miss Scarlet!" gasped Mrs. White. "You look so beautiful."

"Well, don't sound so surprised!" snapped Miss Scarlet. "I *always* look beautiful! Take my bag. And be careful with it. It's filled with gold coins from one of my many rich admirers."

Mrs. White nodded with a smile that changed to a scowl when Miss Scarlet's back was turned. She lugged the heavy suitcase to Miss Scarlet's room. As it happened, the suitcase was black leather, and identical to Colonel Mustard's.

The moment Mrs. White dropped the suitcase next to Miss Scarlet's bed, the doorknocker knocked again. She raced downstairs. The be-spectacled Professor Plum stood outside in a purple coat, purple bow tie, and purple polka-dot underwear.

"Um, ah, Professor," began Mrs. White, reddening. "You seem to have forgotten your pants."

Plum looked confused. "Not at all," he said. "They're in my suitcase."

Mrs. White stared at the suitcase. It was made of black leather. In fact, it looked exactly like Colonel Mustard's and Miss Scarlet's. Professor Plum waited for Mrs. White to carry the suitcase away.

"Don't worry," the maid told him. "I won't take your suitcase. I promise."

"You won't take my suitcase?" asked the Professor. "That's rather odd. Why won't you?"

"Well," said Mrs. White, "I just thought you might have priceless valuables in there or something."

"No, no," said Plum. "My pants were on sale." Then a puzzled look crossed his face. "Come to think of it, I can't remember what else is in there."

He handed the black suitcase to Mrs. White. Her arm nearly fell off as the suitcase crashed to the floor.

"Ah, yes, now I remember what's inside," said Plum. "Fossils."

"Fossils?" asked Mrs. White.

"Yes, a big batch of rare rocks I found on a

recent dig. So rare, in fact, that they're worth over a million dollars."

"Shall I have Mr. Boddy put them in the safe?"

"No, I'd rather keep the suitcase with me, if you don't mind," Plum said. "Put it in my room."

"Right," agreed Mrs. White. It took her twenty minutes to drag the suitcase to the Professor's room. Then she hurried back to the Hall to answer the door again.

This time it was Mr. Green. He was wearing a cucumber-green coat, a pepper-green tie, and an olive-green hat.

"Now that's what I call dressing," said Mrs. White, complimenting Green's green clothes. "*Salad* dressing," she added under her breath.

Unfortunately, Mr. Green heard her. "Don't insult me again," he grumbled. "Or I'll — " He raised a Wrench in the air.

"You'll what?" said Mrs. White, holding up the Candlestick.

"No fighting, please," begged Mr. Boddy as he rushed back into the Hall. Mr. Green and Mrs. White slowly lowered their weapons.

"Here, take my bag, would you?" Mr. Green told Mrs. White. "And be sure you put it in the right room. It's only got about a million dollars worth of stocks and bonds in it."

Mrs. White nodded and dragged the suitcase from the Hall. As luck would have it, the suitcase was black leather, just like the others.

7

Mrs. Peacock was the last guest to arrive. She smiled at Mrs. White as the maid opened the door. Mrs. White didn't know she was smiling, though. Mrs. Peacock's blue coat was modestly buttoned up to her forehead.

After Mrs. Peacock had undone the buttons, she handed Mrs. White her black leather suitcase. By sheer chance, the suitcase looked exactly like all the others. Mrs. Peacock handed over the bag, and the contents shifted slightly, with a *chink* of glass and a *slosh* of liquid.

"What's inside?" asked Mrs. White, arching one eyebrow in surprise.

"What's inside?" Mrs. Peacock blushed blue. "Oh, dear, I'm afraid I can't tell you. It . . . it wouldn't be proper to say the word aloud."

Mrs. White shrugged. "Of course." She smiled politely, then turned away and rolled her eyes as she carried Mrs. Peacock's bag to her room.

Meanwhile, outside the mansion, darkness began to fall.

Within a few hours . . .

Within a few hours, it was pitch dark. The guests were asleep, and all was quiet at Mr. Boddy's mansion. Too quiet.

Then a floorboard creaked.

And creaked again.

One of Mr. Boddy's guests was tiptoeing through the hallway toward Mr. Green's room. In one hand the guest carried a black leather suitcase.

The guest found Mr. Green sleeping with his black suitcase clutched in his arms.

Gently, the guest pried Mr. Green's fingers loose from the bag, pulling one finger at a time.

Luckily, Mr. Green didn't wake up . . .

But, when the guest tried to pry the last finger away, Mr. Green suddenly stopped snoring. "Stop, Mama!" he shouted. "Please don't take my toy!"

The guest waited. Soon Mr. Green started snoring again, and the guest carefully switched the bags. Mr. Green grasped the new bag tightly.

"Thank you, Mama," he murmured dreamily.

"You're quite welcome," the thief told him with a sneer.

One minute later . . .

One minute later, Mrs. White tiptoed into Miss Scarlet's bedroom. As it happened, Mrs. White was carrying a black leather suitcase of her own. *This* bag was also identical to all of the others. Mrs. White used it to store her extra feather dusters.

"I hate to part with my feather dusters," she

9

whispered to the sleeping Miss Scarlet. "But I've decided to swap my bag for your gold coins. Call me crazy!"

She smiled wickedly. But when she began to search the room, her smile faded fast. Miss Scarlet's black bag was nowhere to be found.

"Where did you hide it, you vain thing?" the maid muttered. She slowly opened the closet door, trying to keep it from squeaking. Inside hung thirty expensive scarlet dresses. But no black bag.

Mrs. White glanced at Miss Scarlet. She was still sleeping peacefully, her head resting on a large black pillow.

A black pillow?

Mrs. White did a double take. Miss Scarlet was sleeping on her suitcase!

Mrs. White thought for a moment. Then she crouched down behind the headboard. She reached into the pocket of her white nightgown and found a bobby pin. She threw the bobby pin at the window. It rapped against the glass.

"Who's there!" demanded Miss Scarlet, sitting bolt upright in bed.

Seeing no one, Miss Scarlet settled right back down and fell asleep again. Her head once again rested on the black leather suitcase. But it wasn't the *same* black leather suitcase. Mrs. White had switched the bags.

At the exact same instant that Miss Scarlet sat

bolt upright in bed, Professor Plum sat bolt upright in *his* bed. "I've just remembered something," he said aloud. "My fossils are worth less than a million. In fact, they're just plain worthless!"

Then he remembered something else. He remembered that Mr. Green's suitcase was filled with a million dollars worth of stocks and bonds. He tiptoed into Green's room, pried Green's fingers loose, and switched the bags.

Then Professor Plum tiptoed backward out of Mr. Green's room, carrying the black leather suitcase.

At the same time, Mrs. White tiptoed backward out of Miss Scarlet's room, carrying the black leather suitcase she had just stolen. Both Plum and White tiptoed quietly. They didn't make a sound. But they tiptoed right into each other!

The two thieves screamed and dropped their bags.

"Why don't you watch where you're going!" cried the Professor, grabbing one of the suitcases.

"Sorry, sir," mumbled Mrs. White, grabbing the other suitcase.

"What are you doing up so late?" demanded Professor Plum.

"I . . . I couldn't sleep," the maid stammered. "So I went for a little walk."

"With a suitcase?"

"Er, yes. I thought it might be a *long* walk."

11

Then she saw the suitcase in the Professor's hand. "But what about you? What are *you* doing up so late with a suitcase?"

The Professor thought quickly. "The same reason as you. Good night!" He headed for his room.

But he had taken the wrong bag.

Mrs. White headed for her room as well. But all the arguing had finally roused Mr. Green. When Mrs. White turned the corner, she bumped right into him.

Mr. Green was holding the Wrench. He closed it on Mrs. White's nose. "Give me back my bag or your nose will never run again," he growled.

"Bud id's nod your bag," said the maid in a pinched nasal voice.

"Do you have a cold?" Mr. Green asked.

"No, id's duh Wrench."

"Oh." Mr. Green kept the Wrench on her nose, however, as he snatched the suitcase. He flicked it open. Inside the suitcase lay bottle after bottle of blue mouthwash, ten in all. "What?! This isn't my bag!"

"Thad's whad I'b been drying to dell you," said Mrs. White.

Mr. Green's angry face collapsed into tears. "I'm ruined!" he blubbered. "Ruined!"

WHO STOLE MR. GREEN'S SUITCASE?

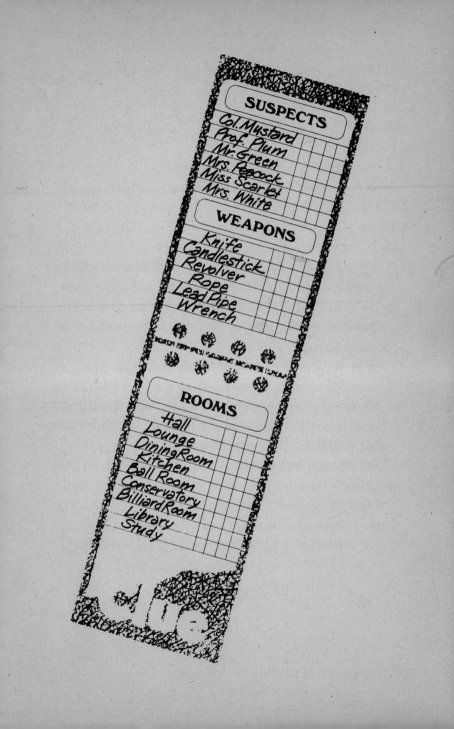

SOLUTION

MRS. PEACOCK

After the first swap, we don't know what's in Mr. Green's new suitcase. But we can keep track of it. Professor Plum took Mr. Green's new bag. Then he bumped into Mrs. White, who took his bag by mistake. So then she had the telltale bag. When Mr. Green opened this bag, he found blue mouthwash. That means that the unknown guest who made the first swap with Mr. Green had mouthwash in his or her bag.

There are six identical suitcases. We know what's in every suitcase but one. Mrs. Peacock refused to say what was in her bag because she thought it wasn't proper. Mrs. Peacock was embarrassed to discuss mouthwash in public. But she wasn't embarrassed to steal Mr. Green's bonds!

2.
Cut Down to Size

"**A**HHHHHH," SIGHED MR. BODDY. "Now this is the life."

He was lounging — in the Lounge, of course — in his bathrobe. His slippered feet rested on a soft footrest. In one hand he held a section of the Sunday *Little Falls Gazette*. In the other hand he held a steaming mug of coffee, filled to the brim. Playing on the record player was his favorite song, "Twinkle Twinkle Little Star."

For the moment, everything was perfect.

For the moment . . .

"Good morning, Mr. Boddy," sang his maid, Mrs. White, as she bustled into the room in a white bathrobe. She was smiling broadly. "More coffee?"

"Yes, thank you," mumbled Boddy.

Mrs. White poured, smirking slyly.

Mr. Boddy let out a scream. Since there was no room left in the already full cup, the extra coffee had poured all over his hand.

"Sorry," said Mrs. White, scowling. "How stupid of me." But when Mr. Boddy went back to reading, her scowl changed into a smile. She bustled out.

"Reginald, darling!" exclaimed Miss Scarlet as she sailed into the room. She was wearing red silk pajamas and clutching a bright red teddy bear. She stretched like a cat, yawned, and screamed.

Mr. Boddy threw his paper up in the air.

"Sorry," said Miss Scarlet with a laugh, "just clearing my throat."

"Oh. Well, that's all right. Make yourself at home." Mr. Boddy returned to reading.

"Oh, my, what a beautiful morning!" Miss Scarlet rushed across the room and flung the windows open wide. The cold breeze started turning the pages of the paper in Boddy's hand.

"Ah, perhaps we shouldn't open the window quite so wide, Miss Scarlet," Mr. Boddy said. "I'm feeling a bit — "

Miss Scarlet turned and screamed at the top of her lungs again.

"You know, Miss Scarlet, perhaps you should drink something. I find that when *I* have a tickle in my throat, the — "

"You scoundrel!" cried Miss Scarlet. She reached into the pocket of her pajamas and pulled out a Knife.

"Er, what did I do this time?" asked her confused host.

Miss Scarlet was slowly coming closer. She held the Knife over Boddy's head.

16

Then she stabbed.

But she didn't stab Mr. Boddy. She stabbed the newspaper. She was cutting out a clipping.

"Um, Miss Scarlet," Mr. Boddy began. "I'm still reading the paper, actually."

"I only want this wedding announcement," Miss Scarlet explained. "John Hartzbreaker is an old flame of mine, the traitor!"

Mr. Boddy kept protesting, but to no avail. And just then, Mr. Green shuffled into the room in his celery-green bathrobe and lime-green slippers. He rubbed his eyes, then shrieked. "Coupons!" He took out a Knife and started stabbing Boddy's paper as well.

Then Colonel Mustard ran into the room, did twenty jumping jacks, beat his breast ten times, and yodelled. "Hallelujah!" he said. "I'm up." Then he saw Miss Scarlet and Mr. Green stabbing Mr. Boddy's paper. He moved closer.

"Duel in the Sun!" he shouted. He pulled out a Knife and joined in the stabbing as he tried to cut out the movie listing.

Plum was next, in his purple bathrobe. "Memory aids!" he gasped, peering at the paper. "I've been meaning to order these tapes, but I keep forgetting." He used his Knife to cut out the ad.

"I hope you're cutting out all the dirty words!" huffed Mrs. Peacock, when she saw what was going on. She started using her Knife to cut out

17

words such as slime, sludge, and filth, slipping the clippings into the pocket of her blue robe.

"Stop! Stop!" begged Boddy. "Mrs. White!" he cried, as his maid entered the room. "Please help!"

Instead, Mrs. White pulled out a Knife and began cutting out a household hints article entitled, "Thirty Uses for Arsenic around the Home."

"Everyone out!" Mr. Boddy roared.

"Why, Mr. Boddy," said Miss Scarlet. "I've never heard you raise your voice that way."

"That's true," agreed all the guests. Then they all went back to stabbing the paper. Finally, they were done. The guests filed out of the room, studying their clippings. At last, all was quiet.

Mr. Boddy looked at the paper in his hands. It now looked like Swiss cheese. His heart was pounding.

Mr. Boddy gritted his teeth. Then he took a deep breath. Slowly, he began to calm down. Ten minutes later, he was absorbed in his paper, humming happily along with the music. "Twinkle, twinkle, little star," he sang to himself. "How I wonder why Miss Scarlet is screaming."

Mr. Boddy put the paper down. "Why *is* Miss Scarlet screaming?"

"Mr. Boddy," gasped Mrs. White, running into the room. "Miss Scarlet just found Colonel Mustard in the Ball Room. He's been murdered!"

In the Ball Room, Colonel Mustard sat slumped in a chair, his copy of the Sunday paper draped over his lifeless body.

"He's been stabbed with a Knife," said Mr. Green, after examining the Colonel's wounds.

"How rude," said Mrs. Peacock.

Just then, Mr. Boddy rushed into the room, followed by Mrs. White. Mr. Boddy took one look at the corpse, then covered his face with his hands and began to blubber.

"Who would do such a wonderful — I mean horrible — thing?" gasped Mrs. White.

"Don't look at *me*," said Miss Scarlet.

"All right," said Professor Plum. He turned and gazed at the wall.

"Well," said Mrs. Peacock. "I know one thing. The murderer is in this room."

"But who had a motive?" asked Green.

"Yes, good question," said Miss Scarlet. "Who hated Mustard?"

"I've always thought it was good on hot dogs," mumbled Plum.

Mr. Boddy, meanwhile, was pulling the papers off Mustard's body.

"Will you look at that," said Mrs. White. "I guess nothing can keep Mr. Boddy from reading his Sunday papers."

"Quiet," said Mr. Boddy. He flipped through the newspaper briskly. There were pieces cut out of the wedding page, the household hints page, and the food coupons page.

"Sure," said Mrs. White. "That's what's important. For us to be quiet while you read your papers. Never mind that a man's been killed and his murderer is on the loose."

"Not on the loose," said Boddy slowly. "The killer is indeed in this room, and I know from my own recent experience how this murder occurred. It was an accident, you see."

"An accident?" Mrs. Peacock chuckled. "Oh, Mr. Boddy, you're so trusting. Who would walk up to the Colonel and stab him in the chest by accident?"

"Someone who wanted to cut out a clipping from Mustard's paper," said Boddy, holding up the shredded newspaper. "Apparently, the murderer slipped while he or she clipped and . . ."

He gestured to the Colonel. "This is the terrible result."

Meanwhile, Mr. Green was strolling casually toward the door.

"Going somewhere?" Miss Scarlet asked him.

"Yes, I'd love to stick around, but I've got an important business appointment."

Mr. Boddy crossed the room and locked the door. "No one's leaving this room," he said. "Not until you let me see those Knives of yours."

The guests all took out their Knives. Mr. Boddy studied them closely. "Hmm," he said, disappointed. "Not a trace of blood on any one of them."

"There goes that theory," said Plum.

"Not necessarily," said Mr. Boddy. "The killer must have wiped the Knife off on his or her robe."

Everyone stared closely at everyone else's robe. At first glance, there didn't appear to be blood on anyone's clothes.

"In that case," said Mr. Boddy. "I will now name the murderer."

WHO KILLED COLONEL MUSTARD?

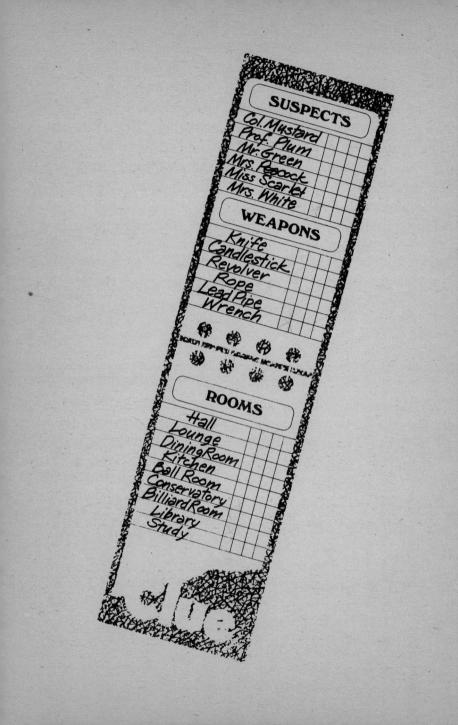

SOLUTION

MISS SCARLET in the BALL ROOM with the KNIFE

The three clippings from Mustard's paper narrow our list of suspects down to Green, White, and Scarlet. But no blood was readily visible on anyone's robe or pajamas. Only Miss Scarlet's red silk pajamas would hide the telltale clue.

By the way, after the guests solved the mystery, it occurred to them to call a doctor. The doctor arrived in time to save the Colonel.

3.
Dressed to Kill

"**M**RS. WHITE!" CALLED MISS SCAR-let, clapping her hands. "My tea, please!"

"Make that two teas, Mrs. White," added Mrs. Peacock.

"Three," said Mr. Green.

"Four teas, Mrs. White," ordered Colonel Mustard.

"Six!" called out Professor Plum.

"He means five, Mrs. White," corrected Mr. Green. "I wish she'd get here soon," he muttered to himself.

It was Monday night, and the guests were all gathered for a tea party in the Dining Room at Mr. Boddy's mansion. But so far no one had seen hide nor hair of Mrs. White.

Now the doors opened. A maid in a black dress and white apron entered, wheeling a silver cart.

At least it looked like a maid. But then the figure raised its head.

"Mr. Boddy!" cried all the guests. "What on earth!"

"It's Mrs. White's night off," explained their host. His eyes twinkled merrily. "I thought I'd surprise you."

Colonel Mustard guffawed. Mrs. Peacock sniffed, "It's vulgar. Take that dress off at once."

"Why? I think he's the best dressed one in the room," said Mr. Green.

"You're joking," said Miss Scarlet.

"I'm serious," Mr. Green insisted.

Miss Scarlet jumped to her feet. "Take that back, you ignorant buffoon!" She yelled the words at Mr. Green. "Admit *I'm* the best dressed!"

Mr. Green leaped up. He was waving the Wrench in his hand.

"Please, please," cried Mr. Boddy. He ran forward but tripped on his maid's dress and fell flat on his face.

"Actually," said Plum, admiring his own outfit, "I think *I'm* the best dressed one here."

"Don't *you* start," said Miss Scarlet. "Or I'll — "

"You'll what?" demanded Plum. He pulled his left hand out of his pocket. There was nothing in it. He looked annoyed. Then he pulled out his right. This hand held the Knife. He raised his left hand high and said, "Don't push me too far!"

Mr. Boddy had gotten to his feet again. "Please, please, no fighting, I beg you. You're *all* dressed wonderfully."

But by then, fighting had broken out on all

sides. A blow struck Boddy on the back of the head. The host fell back to the floor. And he didn't wake up again until . . .

The next morning . . .

"Oomph," grunted Mrs. White. She was straining to tie a tight knot around a tree on the edge of Mr. Boddy's lawn. "There!"

She had hung up the Rope to use as a clothesline. Now she started hanging up the laundry.

It was odd. She hadn't seen a soul since she arrived at the mansion an hour earlier.

Just then, the front door opened. Mr. Boddy emerged and made his way across the sloping lawn toward Mrs. White. At first he seemed to be wearing a white hat. When he got closer, she saw that his head was wrapped in a bandage. "Hello, Mrs. White," he said. "Beautiful day, isn't it?"

"Yes," agreed the maid. "But what happened to you?"

"Nothing to worry about. Feather dance peanut trumpet."

"I'm sorry?" asked the maid.

"No, *I'm* sorry," said Mr. Boddy, tapping his head. "I've been having a little bit of trouble talking straight this morning. Last night's dinner party got a little umbrella, I'm afraid."

"Oh?"

"Yes, I'm afraid the elephant banana garbage noodle."

He tapped his head again. "Sorry." He tried again. "I'm afraid that the guests started arguing about who was the best dressed and . . ." He waved a hand and said, "You can probably imagine the pancake that *that* started."

"I certainly can," said the maid. "I hope no weapons were involved."

"I'm afraid they were," admitted Mr. Boddy. "Each of the guests had one."

"How awful," said Mrs. White.

"Yes. It was. Well, the police will be here any tornado, but I don't know what I can tell them. The events of last night are all a mystery to me. I certainly can't answer the most important question."

"You mean, who *was* the best dressed?"

"No, no," said Mr. Boddy, gently rubbing his sore head. "Who was ducky daddles."

"Right," said Mrs. White. She tapped his head again. "So who *was* the best dressed?"

"I have no sneaker. All I can remember is that Professor Plum was the only guest who wore his own color. And both women's dresses were lovely, but beyond that, it's all an utter marshmallow. Well, I'm going to go lie down and see if I can clear my pineapple before the police get here. They'll of course want to know who was nickel pickle."

27

"Yes, I'm sure they will. You have no idea who attacked whom?"

"That's what I've been trying to remember," said Mr. Boddy with a frown. "But all I know is that the women attacked the women and the men attacked the men. Well, I better cracker!"

With that, he hobbled off.

Mrs. White thought for a moment, but she didn't see any way to help Mr. Boddy solve the mystery. Then she hung up the rest of the laundry, and the events of the previous night suddenly became clear to her.

Because . . .

First she hung a scarlet-red dress that was riddled with bullet holes.

Then she clothespinned up a mustard shirt that had been slit by a Knife.

Next came a green pair of pants with wrinkles that looked as if they had been wrenched by a Wrench.

Then there was the peacock-blue gown with scorch marks, that looked as if it had been burned by the candle in the Candlestick.

A pair of plum-purple slacks had no crease, as if they had been rolled out with the Lead Pipe.

Mrs. White gazed at the clothes as they flapped in the stiff breeze. Which guest was wearing which outfit? she wondered.

Then suddenly, she had the answer.

To solve the mystery, first figure out:

WHO WAS WEARING WHAT?

And then see if you can figure out:

WHO ATTACKED WHOM?

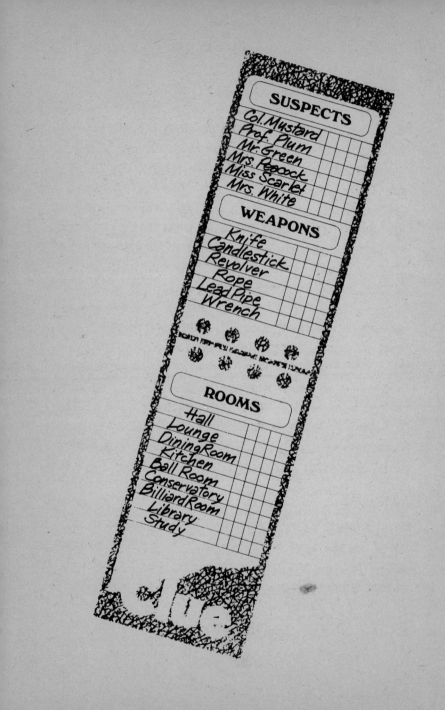

SUSPECTS

Col. Mustard			
Prof. Plum			
Mr. Green			
Mrs. Peacock			
Miss Scarlet			
Mrs. White			

WEAPONS

Knife			
Candlestick			
Revolver			
Rope			
Lead Pipe			
Wrench			

ROOMS

Hall			
Lounge			
Dining Room			
Kitchen			
Ball Room			
Conservatory			
Billiard Room			
Library			
Study			

clue

SOLUTION

MRS. PEACOCK was wearing the Scarlet dress; MISS SCARLET was wearing the peacock-blue gown; PLUM was clad in the purple slacks; MR. GREEN wore a mustard shirt; and COLONEL MUSTARD had on the green pants.

We know this because we know that only Plum wore his own color, and both women wore dresses. So, for example, the mustard shirt had to be worn by one of the other two men. And since Mustard couldn't be wearing mustard, it must have been Mr. Green.

Now we know who was wearing what. We also know that the men attacked the men, while the women attacked the women.

Therefore, Miss Scarlet attacked Mrs. Peacock with the Revolver; Mrs. Peacock attacked Miss Scarlet with the Candlestick; Professor Plum attacked Mr. Green with the Knife; Mr. Green attacked Colonel Mustard with the Wrench; and Colonel Mustard attacked Plum with the Lead Pipe.

Boddy tells us that Plum had the Knife. Since Mr. Green's shirt was slit by a Knife, Plum attacked Green. Boddy also tells us that Green had the Wrench, which by the same reasoning process gives us the final two pieces of the puzzle.

By the way, only Mr. Boddy was injured in the argument. The guests attacked each other's clothes after the guests themselves had changed into new outfits. Only the clothes were hurt!

4.
Charades

"**T**WEET TWEET! TWEET TWEET!" PROfessor Plum flapped his wings like a bird as he fluttered around the Lounge.

"Bird!" shouted the other members of his charades team. Plum tapped his nose proudly with his forefinger. Bird was correct.

"One minute left," called Mr. Boddy, who was studying his stopwatch. This was turning out to be a very close game of charades. Professor Plum's team was in the lead. But now Professor Plum appeared to be lost in thought.

"Give us another clue!" yelled one of his teammates.

Plum shrugged helplessly.

"Shrugging helplessly!" guessed his other teammate.

Plum shook his head no.

"Shaking your head no!" guessed the first teammate.

Plum looked blank.

"Huh?" guessed the second teammate.

Plum shook his head again.

Then both of his teammates cried out at the same time. "You forgot the clue!"

Plum tapped his nose happily. They got it right that time.

"Thirty seconds left!" yelled Mr. Boddy.

"How could you forget the clue?!" yelled his teammates. Plum shrugged one last time, then waved good-bye as he headed back toward his team.

"Bye-bye!" guessed one of his teammates.

"Bye-bye Birdy!" called out the other.

"That's right!" Mr. Boddy called, stopping his stopwatch. "The movie is *Bye-Bye Birdy.*"

"*Bye-Bye Birdy!*" cried Professor Plum, slapping his forehead. "That's it!"

"Yes," said Boddy. "That's what I just said. Let's see. You guessed it in just one minute and forty-nine seconds."

"What's the score?" asked Mrs. Peacock, the other team's captain.

Mr. Boddy studied his scoresheet. "Professor Plum's team is still in the lead. But your team has one last turn. To win, you'll have to guess your final movie clue in less than . . . thirty seconds."

"Thirty seconds?" Professor Plum chuckled. "Impossible!"

"Perhaps," said one of his teammates. "But look whose turn it is."

Mrs. Peacock was now reaching into the hat to pull out the final clue. Mrs. Peacock was not only her team's captain. She was also the best charades player among all of Mr. Boddy's guests. If anyone could pull out a victory, it was she.

Unless . . .

Professor Plum had his hands in his pockets. One of those hands now tightened around the Knife.

Mrs. Peacock studied the scrap of paper on which the clue was scribbled. "Oh, dear, this is a hard one," she said.

"Time to begin," Mr. Boddy called, clicking his stopwatch.

Mrs. Peacock waved her hands in the air, making a circle.

"Whole idea," guessed Colonel Mustard.

Mrs. Peacock tapped her nose to show that this was correct, then she began skipping around the room like a little girl.

One of the members of Professor Plum's team now quietly drew out a Revolver. But Colonel Mustard saw her do it. Behind his back he now pulled out a Lead Pipe. If there was going to be any fighting, he would defend his team.

Meanwhile, Mrs. Peacock had dropped to the floor and was barking like a little dog. Then she got back to her feet and began to spin around the room like a tornado. Her teammates stared at her, utterly mystified.

"Fifteen seconds left," called Mr. Boddy.

Mrs. Peacock was spinning close to Professor

Plum's team. Just then, someone on Plum's team turned off the lights.

There was a dull thud. Then the lights came back on.

Mrs. Peacock was still spinning. But now she clutched her head with both hands.

"Headache!" cried Mrs. White.

Mrs. Peacock shook her head. She pointed at the opposing team.

"Pointing!" guessed Colonel Mustard.

Mrs. Peacock rubbed her head and said, "Ow."

"No talking," warned Mr. Boddy.

Then Mrs. Peacock fell to the floor.

"Fainting!" guessed Colonel Mustard.

"Give us a new clue!" urged Mrs. White.

But Mrs. Peacock didn't move. She didn't speak. She didn't even breathe.

Suddenly, Mrs. White screamed. She ran to her captain's side.

"She's dead," said Mrs. White with a moan.

"I guess we lose," said the Colonel sadly.

"Oh, no; oh, no," sobbed Boddy. "Who would want to hurt poor Mrs. Peacock?"

While the other guests gathered around Mrs. Peacock, the guilty one managed to sneak the murder weapon — the Candlestick — back up on the mantel.

"I guess I'd better call the police," said Mr. Boddy sadly.

"Wait a minute!" exclaimed Mrs. White. "I've just figured out the mystery!"

The guests all waited.

"It's *The Wizard of Oz!*" shouted the maid.

Mr. Boddy looked confused. "Why would the Wizard of Oz want to hurt Mrs. Peacock?"

"No, no, no," said Mustard. "She means that's the final movie clue."

"You're right," said Boddy. "But there's something more important to figure out here, don't you think?"

"What's that?" asked Professor Plum innocently.

"Who killed Mrs. Peacock!" cried Mr. Boddy.

"That's easy," said Mrs. White. "I've already figured it out. Since each of us had only one weapon, I know exactly who the murderer is."

She turned slowly toward the opposing team. Then she raised her finger in the air and pointed. "You!"

WHO KILLED MRS. PEACOCK?

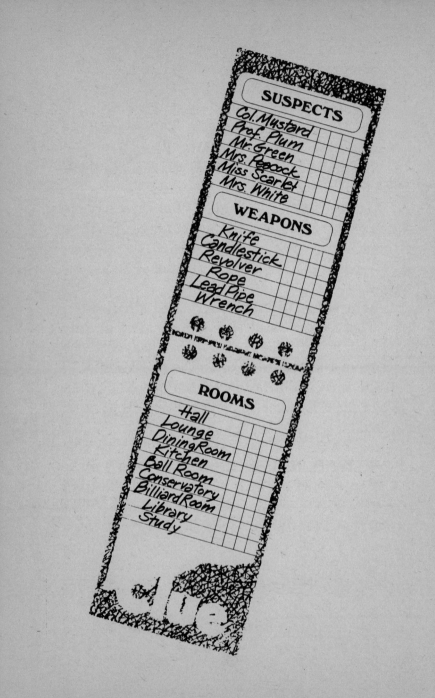

SOLUTION

MR. GREEN with the CANDLESTICK in the LOUNGE

We know — by process of elimination — that Plum's teammates were Mr. Green and Miss Scarlet. Plum had the Knife. Colonel Mustard saw a "her" take out the Revolver. That leaves Green with the murder weapon, the Candlestick.

Luckily, in the dark, Mr. Green's aim was off. He delivered only a glancing blow. Mrs. Peacock woke up a moment later. And when Mr. Boddy awarded the charades victory to her team, all was forgiven.

5.
Bad Taste

"**P**ANCAKES!" ANNOUNCED MRS. White, smiling sweetly. She rolled the silver serving tray into the Dining Room and began serving breakfast to the sleepy guests. But every time she turned back to the cart, her smile changed into an angry grimace.

"Great griddles!" exclaimed Colonel Mustard with his mouth full.

"Mrs. White makes the finest flapjacks in the world," agreed Mr. Boddy, happily shovelling in a large forkful.

"I'll have seconds, if you don't mind," said Mrs. Peacock, daintily wiping her lips with a napkin as she shoved her plate forward.

"Of course," said Mrs. White with a smile. She turned back to the cart, frowned, then turned back and served Mrs. Peacock with a smile.

But no sooner had she served Mrs. Peacock than Miss Scarlet wanted more. Then Professor Plum handed over his empty plate. Then Mr. Green. "Thirds!" cried Mrs. Peacock, handing her plate back again.

40

In short, the guests were going crazy for Mrs. White's pancakes. The pancake tower on her serving cart was growing shorter and shorter. But the guests kept asking for more, more, more. They were eating the pancakes faster than Mrs. White could serve them.

And as she turned faster and faster from the cart to the table, she had to change her smile into a scowl and back again more and more quickly. Soon she got so confused that she was smiling while her back was turned and grimacing when she was facing the guests.

"Mrs. White?" asked Mustard, wiping syrup off his cheek. "Is there anyhing wrong?"

"Not at all," said Mrs. White with a sweet smile and her back turned. Then she whipped around with an angry scowl and muttered directly to the guests, "Except that I'm sick of serving you buffoons."

" 'Buffoons' is a rude word and beneath you," commented Mrs. Peacock with her mouth full. "Perhaps you're overworked."

"But I love my job," said Mrs. White loudly with a smile, while facing her cart. Then she whirled back with a grimace and mumbled, "It's idiots like you that I can't — "

She froze mid-sentence, suddenly aware of her mistake. A smile and a scowl rapidly changed places on her face. Then she fainted.

*   *   *

41

When she came to, she found herself lying on the sofa in the Ball Room. She looked around the room. It was empty. Then she heard the sounds of glasses clinking and laughter tinkling. She slowly got to her feet. The sounds were wafting their way from the Kitchen. She followed the noise.

"Won't she be surprised!" she heard a voice say.

A smell of smoke and something else — skunk? — entered Mrs. White's nose. She yanked open the Kitchen door.

There were pots and pans everywhere. Mixing bowls, open cookbooks, cereals, meats, vegetables, cutting boards, batters, soups, rising bread dough, and three live turkeys cluttered the room.

Each guest was wearing a different color chef's hat. They all looked at Mrs. White with guilty faces. "What is going on?" she asked, holding her head and starting to sway.

Miss Scarlet caught her elbow. "We wanted to surprise you."

"We decided you've been working too hard," added Colonel Mustard. He flipped an omelette, and it landed with a splat on top of Mr. Green's tall green chef's hat.

"We're making *you* lunch," said Mr. Green, ignoring the omelette. "Go put your feet up."

"What's all the smoke?" Mrs. White asked, trying not to breathe too deeply.

"Gobble, gobble," answered one of the turkeys. It waddled over to the maid and eyed her curiously.

Mrs. Peacock laughed. "Oh, the smell. Yes. Well, you see Miss Scarlet is making Scarlet chicken flambé. Professor Plum started to make it but he was making Kitchen flambé instead."

"And the turkeys?" asked the horrified Mrs. White.

Professor Plum scratched his head under his purple chef's hat. "I thought this recipe called for them," he said, studying a cookbook, "but now I don't see where —"

"I don't either," snapped Mr. Green. "Since when does a recipe for stewed plums call for live turkeys?"

"Everything will be fine," Colonel Mustard said, taking the maid firmly by the arm. He led her from the Kitchen back into the Ball Room. "You just relax and let us serve you."

Two hours later . . .

Two hours later, Mr. Green rang the lunch bell. "My mouth is watering already," Mrs. White told Mr. Boddy as they headed for the Dining Room.

"It certainly smells delicious," agreed Boddy.

"Did you bring the stomach medicine?" the maid added under her breath.

"Do you think three bottles will be enough?" whispered Mr. Boddy.

In the Dining Room, the guests were all lined up in a row behind their dishes. The dishes were all hidden beneath silver lids. Streams of foul-smelling steam were slithering out from each metal dish. The chefs bowed low as Mr. Boddy and Mrs. White entered the room.

"Welcome to the finest meal of your life," boasted Mr. Green.

Then the chefs lifted the lids and began to serve.

"Oh, I think I'll just start with — " began Mrs. White, but Mr. Green dumped a large mound of his green salad onto her plate. And the Professor glopped on three big spoonfuls of his stewed plums. By the time the maid had made it down the line, she had a huge portion of each dish. She sat down slowly.

"Dig in," instructed Colonel Mustard.

"Oh, that's okay," said Mrs. White with a tiny smile. "I'll wait."

Soon everyone had been served and was sitting down, ready to eat.

"This is so exciting," Mr. Boddy said. "Now who will take the first bite?"

All eyes turned to Mrs. White. "Our guest of honor," said Mrs. Peacock.

Mrs. White took a small taste of everything on

44

her plate. "Mmmm!" She kept humming and nodding her head and waving her hand in appreciation.

Mr. Boddy went next. He tried a spoonful of Plum's stewed plums, which was smeared with Mustard's Mustard. He took a large bite. All the chefs watched him closely. "This is delicious," he said wryly. Then he made an odd face.

"Delicious . . . isn't . . . the . . . word," he finally stammered, reaching for the water pitcher.

Miss Scarlet tried a bite of Green's greens then quickly took a bite of Peacock stew, and even more quickly a bite of her own Scarlet chicken.

Colonel Mustard smeared his own mustard onto a piece of Scarlet chicken and swallowed it happily. Then he, too, grabbed for the water pitcher. But by now, Mr. Boddy had drunk it all. Mustard gasped in agony.

Professor Plum tried the greens and the Peacock stew. Mrs. Peacock sampled the Scarlet chicken and the greens. They both made very funny faces.

Suddenly, Mrs. White leaped to her feet. She was turning blue. Then green. Then every other color in the rainbow. Then she began to make horrible gargling sounds. Then Colonel Mustard and Mr. Boddy leaped to their feet. Their faces began changing colors as well.

The three of them started to stagger around the

room. They looked as if they were about to die.

They were.

For while all of the guest's creations tasted horrible, one was so bad that it was deadly. And only these three had tasted it.

WHICH IS THE DEADLY FOOD?

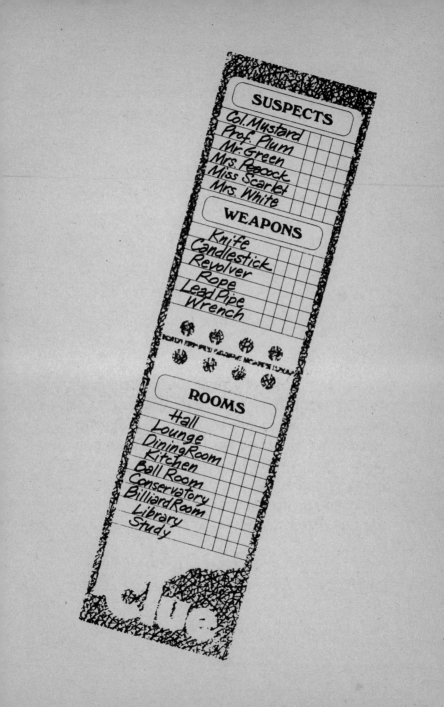

SUSPECTS

Col. Mustard			
Prof. Plum			
Mr. Green			
Mrs. Peacock			
Miss Scarlet			
Mrs. White			

WEAPONS

Knife			
Candlestick			
Revolver			
Rope			
Lead Pipe			
Wrench			

ROOMS

Hall			
Lounge			
Dining Room			
Kitchen			
Ball Room			
Conservatory			
Billiard Room			
Library			
Study			

Clue

SOLUTION

MUSTARD'S mustard made in the KITCHEN and served in the DINING ROOM

We know that only Boddy, Mustard, and Mrs. White had the violent reaction. Boddy had plums and mustard. Mustard had mustard and Scarlet chicken. Only Mustard is on both lists. Mrs. White tasted everything, so she had mustard as well.

Luckily, Mr. Boddy remembered his three bottles of stomach medicine just in time. It saved their lives, but not their appetites!

6.
A Very Important Poison

"**D**O YOU HAVE ANY FIVES, MISS SCAR-let?" asked Mr. Green, studying his cards.

"No," said Miss Scarlet, sneaking a peek at Mrs. Peacock's cards. "Go fish!"

"I think I'm beginning to understand this game," said Mr. Boddy with a jolly smile.

Just then, the Study door opened. Mrs. White pushed in a silver tray laden with six cups of steaming cocoa. She wheeled the tray around the guests, who were sitting on the floor in a circle.

Mrs. White stood behind Mr. Green. She held up three fingers over his head. She winked at Mrs. Peacock.

"Do you have any threes?" Mrs. Peacock asked Mr. Green, winking back at Mrs. White.

Mr. Green frowned, then cleared his throat. "Go fish!" he finally said.

"There's something fishy going on here," Mrs. Peacock grumbled. She reached into the fish pile.

Mrs. White looked at her tray. She had an extra

cup of cocoa. "Where's Professor Plum?" she asked.

"I don't know," said Colonel Mustard. "He was playing with us before, but then I told him to Go Fish and — "

"Oh, dear, yes," said Mrs. White, "I see." She glanced out the window toward the Boddy Pond, but no one was there.

Suddenly, Mrs. Peacock threw down her cards. "Mr. Green is cheating!"

"Oh, yeah?" barked Green, jutting out his jaw in a menacing manner.

Mrs. Peacock jutted out her jaw as well. "Yeah! I mean, Yes!"

Mr. Green crossed his arms over his chest. "Mrs. White's the one who's cheating," he said. "She's giving signals. Don't you *dare* try to pin it on me."

"Well, it's just a card game," began Mr. Boddy. "It doesn't really — "

"Miss Scarlet is cheating, not me," interrupted Mrs. White.

"You mean Colonel Mustard, I believe," said Miss Scarlet, pointing a long finger at the Colonel. "Right, cheater?"

"You dare to accuse me of cheating?" cried Mustard as he leaped to his feet. "I challenge you all to a duel!"

"All of us?" asked Mrs. White. "But Miss Scarlet is the one who accused you."

"Questioning my judgment, eh, Mrs. White? I challenge *you* to a duel!"

"You already did," Mrs. White mocked.

"Mocking me? I challenge you to another duel! And another thing — "

"Ladies, gentlemen, please," interrupted Boddy.

"Interrupting?" said Mustard. "I challenge you, too."

"Mr. Boddy's right, Mustard," said Green. "You shouldn't take the game so seriously."

"I take it too seriously, eh? I challenge you again."

Mrs. Peacock yawned and looked at her watch. "At this rate, he'll be challenging us all night."

Just then, a voice in a far-off room shrieked, "Eureka!"

There was a clatter of footsteps, and Professor Plum rushed into the Study. He was carrying a jar of purple liquid. "Look what I've created!"

The guests looked. "What is it?" they all asked.

"It's . . . it's . . ." Plum stared at the jar of purple liquid in his hand. "I forget what it is!"

The Professor sniffed the liquid, then sipped it. "Ah, yes, now I remember. Poison!"

"Poison!" gasped the guests.

"Yes, poison," said Plum proudly. "I call it Evappo, because once it's inside the body, it evaporates. There isn't the slightest trace of poison left. Don't you see? This is the poison criminals

51

have been searching for. A poison that leaves no clues behind! And just one sip is enough to — "

"Enough to what?" cried Mr. Boddy.

But Professor Plum had gone stiff as a board. He slowly toppled, falling flat on his face.

All the guests rushed to Plum's side. They began to wrestle over the jar of poison clutched in his hand. Colonel Mustard got the jar first, but Mr. Green snatched it away.

"This discovery could be worth millions," said Green.

"Yes!" Miss Scarlet grabbed the jar from Mr. Green. "It's a very important poison!"

"Of course Plum is a very important person," said Boddy, who was trying to revive the Professor. "That's why we've got to help him. Here, give me that!" He pulled the jar away from Miss Scarlet. "I'm going to put this away for safekeeping. In the meantime, someone call a doctor for the Professor!" He ran out of the room.

The guests carried Plum into the Library. Mrs. Peacock called the doctor. The phone rang and rang, but there was no answer. "How rude!" exclaimed Mrs. Peacock as she hung up. The guests propped Plum against the wall.

Meanwhile, Mr. Boddy had hidden the jar of purple poison under the billiard table. "It'll be safe here for the time being," Mr. Boddy told himself. Then he left the room.

He was right. It would have been safe. Except

one of the guests had watched him hide it.

That guest now came out from behind the door, reached under the billiard table, and set the jar of poison on the table's green felt. Next, the guest took out three small darts. "Accuse *me* of cheating," the guest muttered bitterly. "Why, no one accuses me of cheating at 'Go Fish' and lives to tell the tale!"

The guest carefully dipped each of the three darts into the thick, purple liquid.

Meanwhile . . .

"We've got to find it!" cried Mrs. White, looking at Mr. Green. They were in the Lounge, going through the remains of Plum's experiment, hoping to find an antidote for the poison.

The two of them were searching so frantically that they didn't notice that the door that led to the Billiard Room opened slightly. The hollow Lead Pipe nosed into view. It was aimed right at them.

Whoosh!

The guest who was holding the Lead Pipe had just blown one of the purple poison darts through it.

At that same instant, Mr. Boddy burst into the Lounge through the secret passageway from the Conservatory. "Any luck?" he asked, standing in front of Mr. Green and Mrs. White.

Mr. Green and Mrs. White both shook their heads. The poison dart struck Mr. Boddy in the rump.

"Missed!" muttered the guest at the door. The Lead Pipe disappeared from view.

Boddy yelped. He gave Mrs. White an odd look. "Mrs. White!" he said. "One should never pinch one's boss!"

"Thanks for the advice," said Mrs. White, giving him a strange look. "We've been through the whole room, Mr. Boddy. I don't think the Professor invented an antidote for this stuff."

"Well, keep searching," ordered Boddy. Then he rushed to the Study to see how the Professor was doing.

"Oh, Professor Plum," said Boddy. "You're back on your feet again!" Relief spread rapidly over Mr. Boddy's round face. But the Professor, who was leaning against the wall, didn't say a word.

"You gave us quite a scare, let me tell you. But I guess you didn't drink enough of the poison to harm you, eh?"

The Professor still didn't answer.

Suddenly, Mr. Boddy realized the truth. He started backing away as Plum began to fall.

But just then, Boddy himself stiffened up like a board. The two men fell straight over, crashed into each other, and propped each other up like tent poles.

"There's no time to lose, we've got to find that antidote," Mr. Green said as he hurried into the room.

He stopped short when he saw the two frozen men.

"Now that's what I call putting your heads together," said Mrs. White as she entered behind Green.

"Look!" Mr. Green pointed to the dart that was sticking out of Boddy's bottom.

Mrs. White pulled out the dart and examined its purple-stained tip. "Hmm. Looks like we have to find more than antidote," she said.

"Yes," said Mr. Green. "We have to find the killer."

WHO KILLED MR. BODDY?

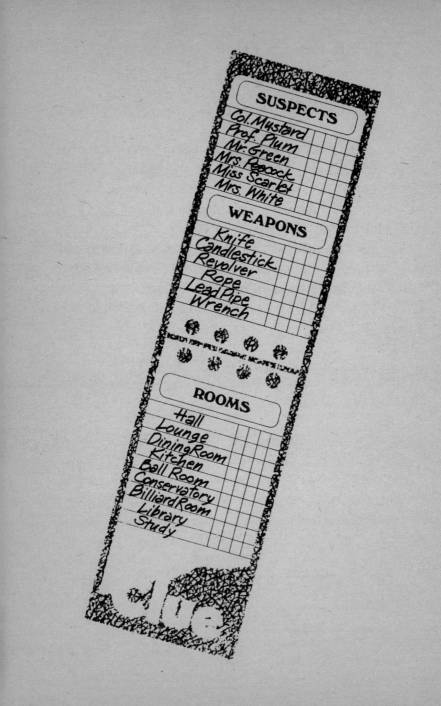

SOLUTION

MISS SCARLET outside the LOUNGE with the LEAD PIPE

The killer was seeking revenge for being accused of cheating during Go Fish. Miss Scarlet was the only guest outside the Lounge accused by either Mr. Green or Mrs. White.

By the way, Plum really did forget what his discovery was. It wasn't poison at all. It was a sleeping potion. Boddy and Plum woke up an hour later, found themselves leaning against each other, and fell to the floor.

7.
Sound the Alarm!

"**I**T'S ME! OPEN UP!" MR. GREEN STOOD outside the locked front door of Mr. Boddy's mansion, his suitcase at his side. He stamped on the welcome mat, trying to keep warm.

"See if you can break in," instructed Mr. Boddy through the closed door.

"What?"

"See if you can break in," repeated Boddy.

Mr. Green shrugged. Then he took out a credit card. He tried to slide the card into the crack between the heavy wooden door and the metal latch.

It worked. He turned the knob.

But before he could open the door, a piercing siren blasted in his ears. The welcome mat disappeared from beneath Mr. Green's feet as a trapdoor opened. He was falling!

He landed with a crash.

Then his suitcase landed . . . on his head.

Mr. Boddy's round face appeared at the top of the hole. "Just wanted to test out one of my new burglar alarms," he told Mr. Green. "What do you think of it?"

"It works *beautifully*," said Mr. Green. "I'm so glad I decided to *drop* in on you."

Mr. Boddy threw down the Rope. After Green climbed out, Boddy led him to the Study where his other weekend guests were waiting. "Now," Mr. Boddy began, "I have an important announcement to make. I've installed a new security system."

"Yes," said Colonel Mustard, putting on a Band-Aid. "And we all *fell* for it."

"Oh," said Mr. Boddy with delight. "The trap-door in front is only one tiny part of the alarm system. Wait till you see. You'll sleep better, I'm sure, once you see how secure I've made my mansion. But I'd better show you everything right away so you don't set off any false alarms. Walk this way."

The guests all imitated Mr. Boddy's way of walking as he led them into the Study.

"As you can see, the doorway is equipped with electric eyes." He pointed to two glass circles, which had been built opposite each other, about three feet up, in the doorframe.

"Watch this." Boddy inserted a small key above one of the electric eyes. There was a humming sound. Both eyes glowed red.

"Professor Plum," said Mr. Boddy. "Please try

to walk out of the Study through the doorway."

"But I want to watch," said Plum.

"Just do it, please. Trust me."

Professor Plum walked out through the door, breaking the beam between the electric eyes. An alarm sounded, and a heavy metal gate crashed down from the ceiling, blocking the doorway and locking all the guests inside the Study. Boddy turned the tiny key again and the alarm shut off. The gate went back up.

"I've installed these electric eyes and gates in the doorways in all nine first-floor rooms," said Boddy proudly. "Once I've set the alarm for the night, those rooms will be totally secure. You can come back now, Professor!"

But the Professor had forgotten why he had walked out of the room. He didn't return.

"Security cameras," said Mr. Boddy, pointing up at a movie camera installed near the Study ceiling. "Radar." He pointed to a sensor installed near the movie camera. "The radar system, like all of the alarms, is controlled from my bedroom. I can use it to track any first-floor intruders."

He pointed to a speaker that had been built into the wall. "The special security loudspeaker system."

"Very impressive," said Colonel Mustard, "but — "

Mr. Boddy held up a hand. "There's more. All of you tried to break in through the front door.

You failed because of the trapdoor. But let's say a burglar somehow succeeded in opening the front or back door or any window of the mansion. The whole first floor would ooze with glue fired by special nozzles. And the sticky-fingered burglar would find himself or herself quite stuck."

Mrs. Peacock whistled. "A system like this must have cost a pretty penny."

"It cost a lot more than that," said Mr. Boddy.

"But why have you invested in all these precautions?" asked Colonel Mustard. "Are you that afraid of burglars?"

"Because I've got the Lollapaloosa," answered Boddy.

"The famous diamond?" Miss Scarlet's eyes sparkled like twin gems.

"Yes," said Boddy, his voice a mere whisper. "The Lollapaloosa Diamond. The largest diamond in the world."

"What did you say" asked the guests, cupping their hands up to their ears to hear better.

"The Lollapaloosa Diamond," said Boddy loudly. "I bought it last week." He pointed across the room at a painting of some ducks. "I'm keeping it behind there, in the safe."

"Don't you trust us?" asked Miss Scarlet, tickling Mr. Boddy under his chin. At the same time, she slipped the Revolver into her purse.

Mr. Boddy giggled wildly. "Of course I trust you. I would trust you all with my life. These

61

alarms are only to protect us from the rest of the world, which I *don't* trust one bit."

"Good thinking," said Mr. Green. "You can't be too careful nowadays." As he gave this sage advice, he slid the Knife into his pocket.

In the very middle of the night . . .

In the very middle of the night, the burglar alarm began to shriek and whoop. Boddy's radar blipped loudly.

Alarmed, Mr. Boddy sat up in bed. He studied his radar screen. The blip was coming from the Kitchen. The blip moved to the refrigerator.

Boddy reached over to the next console of his burglar alarm control panel and flipped a switch. An image appeared on the dark screen. His security camera showed a tall man in purple pajamas, sipping a glass of milk.

Mr. Boddy turned off the alarm. "Professor Plum," said Boddy into his loudspeaker system.

The Professor looked around, bewildered. "It's Mr. Boddy," said Boddy. "Remember I explained to you that no one could go downstairs after the alarm was set? Please go back to bed."

Boddy hit another switch and the Kitchen's metal gate lifted back up into the ceiling. Professor Plum headed back upstairs, and Mr. Boddy hit the reset button.

Plum paused on the stairs. "My milk!" he

exclaimed. He turned and headed back into the Kitchen. When he broke the beam of the electric eyes, the gate crashed shut behind him again. Again the alarm began to shriek and whoop.

Meanwhile, a masked man was moving quietly down the mansion's long front stairway. When the alarm went off again, he paused, one foot in the air.

"You've done it again, Professor," the masked man heard Boddy call on the loudspeaker system.

The alarm shut off. The masked man continued on his way.

He was carrying a chair. He walked straight to the Study and set the chair down right in front of the doorway. He stood on the chair and leaped.

He cleared the electric beam by several inches.

The masked man removed the duck painting from the wall. Then he pulled a Wrench from his pocket and went to work on the safe's thick metal door.

Just then, someone opened one of the windows on the second floor.

Instantly, the alarm sounded again. The Study floor began to shake. Twelve metal nozzles pushed up through the floor and began spurting thick green glue. The masked man watched in horror.

"My shoes!" he gasped. They were stuck to the floor.

"No matter," the thief told himself. "First I'll get the Lollapalooza. Then I'll think of some way to escape." He resumed his work on the safe door.

"Professor Plum!" Mr. Boddy was calling over the loudspeaker system. "Oh, Professor! Please wake up."

The masked man could barely hear Boddy over the noise of the alarm. As for the Professor, he had fallen asleep at the Kitchen table with his fingers in his ears. Mr. Boddy pressed the reset button, but the alarm continued to sound. The reset button was stuck!

At the same time, the guest who had opened the second-floor window was making a belt out of one end of the Rope. The guest began climbing down the mansion wall. The guest with the Rope was wearing a mask. The guest opened the Study window and jumped into the room.

The guest with the Rope landed with a sticky plop. And stayed there.

"Nice try, Mrs. White," said the masked man with the Wrench.

"I'm not Mrs. White," scoffed the second intruder truthfully.

"Well, stick around anyway," joked the man with the Wrench.

"Help me," pleaded the thief with the Rope.

The masked man didn't answer. He went back to *wrenching* open the safe door.

Meanwhile, the alarm was still shrieking. Mr. Boddy pressed the off button again and again, but it was no use. The noise was so loud it covered the sound of the guest who was banging on the floor above the Study. The guest was using the Lead Pipe to knock a series of holes through the plaster. The holes were in a large circle. The circle was right over the head of the masked man with the Wrench. There were only three holes left to complete the circle.

"You'll never get into the safe that way," the thief with the Rope shouted to the guest with the Wrench. "The door's too thick. Why don't you try the combination?"

"If I knew the combination," hollered the thief with the Wrench, "I would."

Over his head, the guest with the Lead Pipe now had two holes left to go.

"I'll tell you the combination if you help me get unstuck," bellowed the thief with the Rope.

"I'm stuck, too," yelled the thief with the Wrench. "Just tell it to me." He placed his hand on the safe's dial and waited.

"I don't know the combination," admitted the guest with the Rope sadly.

The guest with the Lead Pipe now had one hole left to go.

The thief with the Wrench spun the safe's dial. The situation seemed hopeless.

Until he noticed . . .

Could it be? Yes it was! Mr. Boddy had left the safe just one millimeter ajar!

The thief yanked open the door. There lay the

Lollapaloosa Diamond. Nestled on a red pillow, the gem was the size of a dinosaur egg. "Ahh," sighed the thief. The diamond was so large and shiny it hurt his eyes. He reached for it.

But just then, the guest overhead succeeded in poking the last hole and completing the circle. And the huge circle of plaster landed right on the thief with the Wrench, squashing him flat.

Standing on top of the plaster chunk was a masked guest holding the Lead Pipe. The masked guest stared into the open safe. "Ahh," sighed the guest, reaching for the diamond.

But just then — *KerSPLATTT!* — the guest with the Wrench managed to stand back up.

The guest with the Lead Pipe went flying through the air and stuck headfirst in the glue.

As the guest went flying, the Lead Pipe banged into the safe door. The door slammed shut, and something clicked. The safe was now closed and locked. The Lollapaloosa Diamond was safe and secure.

Mr. Boddy, meanwhile, had just typed "Study" into his control keyboard. He watched the screen, waiting for his security camera to show him the intruder.

WHO ARE THE THREE THIEVES?

66

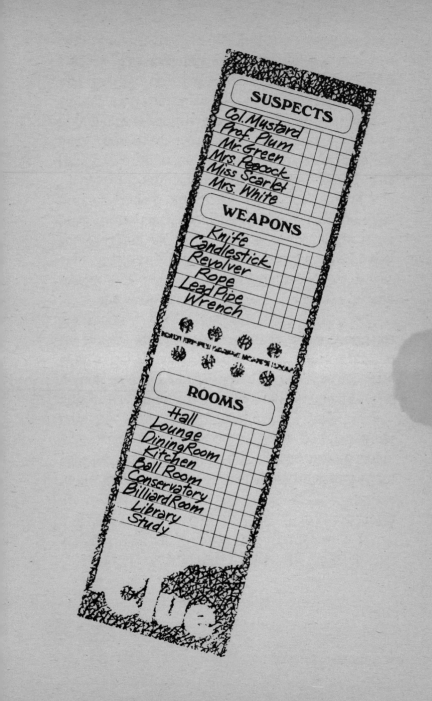

SOLUTION

COLONEL MUSTARD with the WRENCH, MRS. PEACOCK with the ROPE, and MRS. WHITE with the LEAD PIPE, all in the STUDY

We know that Green had the Knife, and Plum was locked in the Kitchen. So the masked man who broke into the Study with the Wrench must have been Colonel Mustard.

We also know that Miss Scarlet had the Revolver, and the guest with the Rope was not Mrs. White. So she must have been Mrs. Peacock, and the guest with the Lead Pipe must have been Mrs. White.

By the way, Mr. Boddy's control screen wasn't working properly. He had actually seen an earlier shot of the Study and thought there was no one there. Then he hit the alarm's automatic reset button one last time, and it finally worked. The nozzles sucked up all the glue. Mr. Boddy and Professor Plum went back to their rooms. The three thieves tried unsuccessfully to crack the safe, then they also went back to bed.

Nobody slept for long. Going for milk again, Plum set off the alarm once more. In the morning, Mr. Boddy returned all the security equipment and sold the Lollapaloosa Diamond.

8.
The Case of the Invisible Cat

"**A**ND NOW," SAID THE RADIO ANNOUN-cer, "here's how our weekend weather forecast is shaping up."

"Oh, dear," mumbled Mr. Boddy. "I hope, I hope — "

What Mr. Boddy was hoping was that he'd have good weather for his weekend polo party. But the announcer continued: "Well, it looks like it's going to be bad weather this weekend for anyone who's planning a polo party! Rain, rain, and more rain."

Disgusted, Mr. Boddy reached out to turn off the radio. But before his hand got to the knob —

The announcer suddenly said, "Oh, no! This just in. . . . Ladies and gentlemen, lock your doors and windows tight. Kitty Lyon, the famous cat burglar, has just escaped from Little Falls Prison!"

Mr. Boddy gasped. "No! I can't believe my ears."

"Yes!" said the announcer. "You'd better be-lieve it. Kitty Lyon, the burglar so stealthy

69

and skillful that they call her the Invisible Cat, has escaped from jail."

"Kitty has escaped! Kitty has escaped!" Mr. Boddy ran through the mansion looking for his guests. "Lock all the doors and windows!"

At the time, all of the guests were gathered in the Lounge. Professor Plum heard Mr. Boddy's warning. He quickly shut and locked the door.

Unfortunately, he shut it just as Mr. Boddy came barrelling into the room. He crashed into the locked door headfirst.

Hearing the awful noise, the guests opened the door, dragged their host into the room and propped him up in the easy chair. "Kitty, Kitty," moaned Boddy, beginning to come to again.

"Quick!" cried Mustard. "Somebody throw that pitcher of cold water on him."

Professor Plum did as he was told.

"No!" yelled Mustard. "I meant the water, not the pitcher, too."

Mr. Boddy was out again. Colonel Mustard began slapping his cheeks. "Kitty, Kitty," Mr. Boddy murmured.

"What's that?" asked the guests. "What are you trying to say?"

"Kitty has escaped!"

"Oh, dear," said Professor Plum. "He's gone bats." He put his mouth to Mr. Boddy's ear and shouted, "Reginald, you don't have a kitty!"

"No, no," said Mr. Boddy, holding his ear in

pain. "Kitty Lyon, the famous cat burglar. She's escaped from jail."

Everyone exchanged worried glances.

"How alarming!" said Miss Scarlet. "And you think she'll come here?"

"Well," said Mr. Boddy, "I am not not not not not the poorest man in town, now am I?"

All of the guests puzzled over this for a moment. With all those negatives, had Mr. Boddy said he was not rich or not poor?

Then Professor Plum said suddenly, "I've got it! If you had said just one 'not' that would have meant you were rich. Two would have meant you were poor, because it would be a double negative. So since you said an *odd* number of 'nots,' you said you were rich."

"And I am," agreed Boddy. "But there is not not not not not not not not not not any time for that now."

Again the guests grew puzzled. "Nope," Mr. Green said finally. "That was ten 'nots,' which is an even number. You're saying there *is* time for that now."

"I think he's having trouble speaking," said Mrs. White. She slapped him on the back.

"Thank you," said Boddy. "I feel much better now. But I'll feel even better when we all have our valuables locked up in the Boddy safe."

"In that case, I'd better change out of this dress," said Miss Scarlet. "It was originally worn by Mata Hari and it's worth a small fortune."

"And this ring is worth a *big* fortune," Mrs. Peacock said. She slipped a large diamond off her finger as Miss Scarlet headed to her room to change.

Colonel Mustard handed Mr. Boddy his Revolver and said, "Here, you'll need this."

"Oh, my goodness," said Mr. Boddy, trembling, "you don't expect me to shoot Kitty, do you?"

"No, no, no," said Colonel. "The bullets are made of gold." He snapped open the gun. Inside, six bullets gleamed yellow. "They're worth six big fortunes."

Miss Scarlet returned wearing a red jumpsuit and carrying the Mata Hari gown over one arm. She handed it over to Mr. Boddy. "Here it is," she said breathlessly.

Professor Plum stared at the dress in Boddy's hands. "I doubt it will fit," he said thoughtfully.

Mr. Green handed Mr. Boddy a large envelope. "Inside information on a few big companies," he whispered.

"Just put it in the safe," Mr. Green said, patting Boddy on the head.

"This is the closest thing I've got to a valuable," Mrs. White said sadly. She handed Mr. Boddy a lottery ticket. "If I win, it'll be worth a million."

"Oh, now, Mrs. White," scolded Mr. Boddy. "How many times have I told you that it's foolish to enter the lottery? Why, the odds of winning are less than the odds of being struck by lightning."

Just then, a bolt of lightning streaked through the dark sky outside the window. It hit the top of the gazebo. "Well," he said, "lightning never strikes twice."

A second bolt hit the gazebo in the exact same place.

"All right," Mr. Boddy said, taking the ticket. "I'll put it in the safe. Maybe you're onto something after all." He added the ticket to his pile of valuables. Then he reached into his pants pocket. "I almost forgot. Petty cash." He pulled out ten packets of cash. Each packet contained a hundred thousand dollar bills.

"But that's a million dollars," said Mrs. White with a gasp.

"Yes," said Boddy. "I always like to have a little money around the mansion. Saves me a trip to the bank. What about you, Professor?"

"I don't mind going to the bank."

"No. I meant, do you have any valuables to lock up?"

"Ah. Just one." Professor Plum handed Mr. Boddy a ballpoint pen.

Mr. Boddy looked at the pen for a moment, turning red. "Ah, Professor, are you sure you remembered what we were talking about?"

Plum scratched his head with a worried frown. "Was it important?"

"Yes! Very! We're locking up our *valuables*."

Plum nodded at the pen in Boddy's hand. "It may not look like much, but I'll wager that that pen is worth more than any of the other valuables put together. It's one of my newest and greatest inventions."

"Ah!" said all the guests at once.

"Ah," added Mr. Boddy, looking at the pen more closely. "What does it do?"

"It writes," said the proud Professor.

Mr. Boddy eyed the Professor strangely. "Yes, well, that's not groundbreaking, but — "

"It writes by itself," explained Plum. He took the pen. "Here, I'll show you."

He took out a blank piece of paper and wrote, *Mr. Boddy is a —* " he paused. "Now. Let's say I get stuck. I just press this little red button on top of the pen and — "

The pen began to move by itself. In an attractive looping style, the pen added the word *ninny*.

"See? *Mr. Boddy is a ninny*. That makes sense, right?" said Plum proudly.

All of the guests clapped, except for Mr. Boddy, who was frowning. Suddenly, the pen began to move again. "Hmm," said Plum. "That's not supposed to happen."

The pen now wrote, *Mrs. Peacock is a fussbudget*.

"How rude!" cried Mrs. Peacock.

Miss Scarlet is a flirt, added the pen. *Mr. Green is a bully. Mrs. White is a —*"

But Plum grabbed the pen before it could write any more. "Obviously, there are still a few bugs in the system which I have to work out, but —"

"It doesn't matter," Mr. Boddy cut him off. "There's no time for this now. We must secure all the valuables at once."

A wave of rain began to fall. The lights flickered and went out. They came back on again almost instantly.

"You see? No time to lose," said Mr. Boddy. "As you all must realize, Kitty Lyon is the world's greatest burglar. She moves fast — and silently — like an invisible cat. Why, she's so hard to spot, she could be on the premises already and we'd never know. And if the lights blow, we'll be completely helpless —"

Suddenly, the pen in Plum's hand began to move again. It scrawled, *Stop talking and put the valuables in the safe.*

"Right," agreed Boddy.

There was the sound of glass breaking.

Danger! the pen wrote on the wall.

"Mr. Boddy, I think we have company," said Mrs. White.

"You're just realizing that now?" asked a confused Professor Plum.

"No, no," said Mrs. White. "I mean, besides the usual guests."

Outside the Lounge, footsteps creaked across the old wooden floorboards.

And then a third bolt of lightning struck. This one hit one of the mansion's twelve gables. The lights flickered again. Only this time they didn't come back on.

In the darkness, the guests heard the Lounge door open. There was a thwack. A scream or two. Lots of running around. Then the sound of the door locking. More running around. Then another thwack. And another. Another. Another. Another.

Three hours later . . .

Three hours later, Professor Plum woke up with a terrible headache. Why is it so dark in here? he wondered.

Then he realized his eyes were still closed. He opened his eyes and a new puzzle presented itself. Where was he?

He peered around the room and saw he was in the basement of Boddy's mansion. Problem solved.

Then a third problem occurred to him. What was he doing in the basement of Boddy's mansion?

I don't remember coming down here, he thought. Well, no matter. I'll go back upstairs.

He tried to move. He couldn't. It seemed that his arms and legs were tied up. He was tied so tightly that he could barely move his head.

"This is awful," he said. He said it aloud, but it came out sounding more like, "Thuh ih awfuh."

Professor Plum had just had another realization. He was gagged.

Just then, he saw something moving on the basement wall a few feet away. His self-writing pen!

Hello, Professor, the pen wrote.

"Hello," he cried in a garbled voice. "What's going on?"

You and the other guests are all tied up, the pen wrote.

The other guests? Plum tried to turn his head but couldn't. But it was true. All the guests were tied together in a bunch. There were muffled groans from all sides. Apparently, the other guests were also starting to revive.

"Who did this?" Plum asked in a muffled voice.

What? wrote the pen.

Plum repeated the question. The pen began to write again. *The person who tied you up is named . . .* The pen kept moving but no more letters appeared. It had run out of ink!

More muffled groans from the other guests. It sounded like everyone else was gagged as well. But Plum was able to communicate a little bit.

First, a voice that sounded like Miss Scarlet or Mrs. Peacock asked if anyone had a Knife so he or she could cut them all free.

77

From the other side of Plum, another voice that sounded like Miss Scarlet or Mrs. Peacock answered. This voice said she had a Knife but couldn't move her hands to use it.

Then a garbled voice suggested that they all try to make their way up the stairs. The voice sounded to Plum like Colonel Mustard or Plum himself.

From the other side of Plum, another voice said this was a great idea. It sounded like Mr. Green or Colonel Mustard.

The tied-up guests began to struggle forward with tiny shuffling steps. The whole group made it to the steps.

"On the count of three," said a garbled voice.

"One . . . two . . . three," chanted the muffled voices of the group. Then they all said, "HOP!"

And the whole bunch of tied-up guests hopped as one, up onto the first stair.

"HOP!"

They made it up to the second stair. "HOP!" The third. In a few minutes, they were only one step away from freedom.

The group rested for a moment. Then the group began counting again.

"One . . . two . . ."

After which, all but one of the group said, "Three! HOP!" And they hopped.

The one member of the group who didn't say this was Professor Plum. What Professor Plum said was, "Oh, dear, would you believe it? I've forgotten what comes after three!"

He also forgot to hop. As a result, the group tripped and rolled back down the stairs.

There were garbled screams. Then silence.

A few minutes later, one of the group announced she had some matches in her pocket. It sounded to Plum like Mrs. White or Mrs. Peacock.

"No thanks," Plum said. "I don't smoke."

But the guest ignored him and struggled to get out the matches. There was the sound of a match being struck. A muffled curse. The sound of another match being struck. This one lit. The guest explained that she was going to try to burn the Rope.

Moments later, Professor Plum smelled smoke. That was just before the other guest had succeeded in burning through the Rope. Unfortunately, by then Plum had forgotten the plan. Thinking quickly, he tried to save the day by rolling over and over on the floor, to put the fire out.

As the whole pile of guests rolled over and over across the basement floor, Mr. Boddy got terribly smushed. It took him several minutes to regain consciousness.

"Now what?" asked a muffled voice.

"Looks like we're stuck here for good," answered another garbled voice.

Then another one of the guests called out in a garbled voice, "I think there are only six of us."

"Isn't that enough?" asked Plum.

"It means," the voice continued, "that one of us is missing." The garbled voice sounded to Plum like Miss Scarlet, Mrs. Peacock, or his mother.

"And whoever is missing," said a second garbled voice, "they must have something to do with taking our valuables and robbing us."

"I've only got one question," said Plum.

"What's that?" asked all the garbled voices at once.

Plum said, "Could you repeat what you just said?"

NAME THE THIEF!

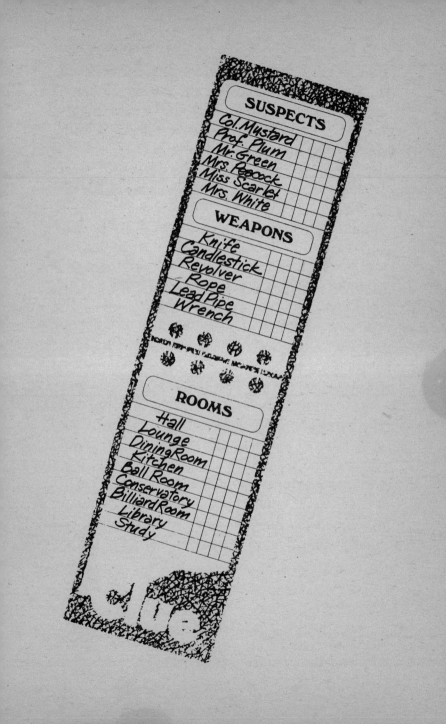

SOLUTION

MRS. WHITE

First of all, we know that Plum is only absent-*minded*. He was certainly present *physically*. So the missing guest can't be Plum.

Then a voice that sounded like Miss Scarlet or Mrs. Peacock called out a question, and a voice that also sounded like Miss Scarlet or Mrs. Peacock answered. That accounts for Miss Scarlet and Mrs. Peacock.

The voice that suggested the guests climb the stairs sounded to Plum like Colonel Mustard or Plum himself. It should be obvious to everyone but Plum that this must be the Colonel. So when Mr. Green or Mustard answered the Colonel, it must have been Mr. Green. Mr. Boddy is the sixth person and is never a suspect. That means the missing person is Mrs. White.

By the way, Mrs. White didn't act alone. She served as an accomplice to the famous escaped cat burglar, Kitty Lyon. But Kitty double-crossed her and made off with all the valuables herself. Still penniless, the bitter Mrs. White returned to the mansion and her duties as Mr. Boddy's maid.

A few hours after that, she set the guests free.

9.
Cloning Around

*"B*ANG! BOOM! ZIP! ZAP! SPLAT! Crunch! Boink! Bing!"*

Mrs. Peacock was on her way to the Billiard Room when she heard these strange sounds coming from the Conservatory. She entered cautiously, and saw —

A large contraption that looked like a cross between an automatic pitching machine and a movie camera. The machine was humming quietly. The strange sounds were coming from Professor Plum, who was talking to himself as he worked.

"Tick! Tock! Kerplunk! Kerplink!" Plum said as he tightened a bolt with the Wrench.

Mrs. Peacock cleared her throat. Plum looked up, startled. "What is *that*?" she asked.

"A Wrench," said Plum, looking at the tool in his hand.

"No, no, no." Mrs. Peacock pointed. "That!"

"That's your forefinger," explained the Professor. "But I'm busy now. You're going to have to figure out some of these questions by yourself."

"No! What is that machine?"

"Ah!" The Professor smiled proudly. "This is a new invention of mine. Amazing, really. Would you believe that this device will make someone instantly smarter?"

"No," said Mrs. Peacock. She inspected the machine closely. "I would *not* believe it."

"Well, then," said Plum. "Allow me to demonstrate. Stand over here."

He placed her in front of the machine's pitching arm and pressed a button.

The machine whirred. Its metal hand closed around a tennis ball, lifted it slowly, and flung it at Mrs. Peacock's head.

She screamed and ducked. The ball sailed out the window and landed right in the middle of Mr. Green's tennis match against Miss Scarlet.

Back in the Conservatory, Mrs. Peacock was fuming. "Is this your idea of a joke, Professor?"

"Sorry," said Plum. "I hit the wrong button. You see, this machine will also serve tennis balls. I designed that part to help Mr. Boddy improve his game."

He pressed another button. The machine whirred again. Now it began projecting a film on the Conservatory wall. The film showed a little baby taking a bath. "That's me!" cried Plum. "Age two!"

Mrs. Peacock let out an impatient sigh and headed for the door.

"Wait!" cried Plum. "I hit the wrong button

again. You see, this machine doubles as a movie projector. But it really works. Watch."

He pressed a third button. Nothing happened.

Once more, Mrs. Peacock started for the door, once more Professor Plum begged her to stay. When that didn't work, he tripped her. "The machine will work perfectly this time, I promise you," he said. "Now, how much smarter would you like to be? Shall we say, five times smarter? . . . Good."

He hurriedly set the dial to five. Then he zapped Mrs. Peacock with a purple beam of light.

"All right," said Plum as he strode around the room. "Let's give you a little test, shall we? Number one. What is the capital of North Kitchymongo? Number two. What is the speed of light divided by the speed of Ketchup when poured from a bottle? Number three. What was Alvin Von Kookoo Klocka's theory of time?" He paused. Mrs. Peacock didn't answer.

"I know they're difficult questions. But now that you're five times smarter, they should seem like a snap to you. Right?"

Plum turned to face his fellow guest. Then he turned again. And again. And again . . .

There were now six identical Mrs. Peacocks standing in the room.

All six Mrs. Peacocks looked outraged. "You fool!" one of the six Mrs. Peacocks cried, looking around at the other Mrs. Peacocks in terror. "What have you done?!"

Professor Plum began to laugh heartily.

"What's so funny?" demanded all the Mrs. Peacocks.

"I'm sorry, I just thought of a silly joke. What did one chicken say to the other — "

The furious look on the faces of all six Peacocks stopped Plum in midsentence. "Sorry." Then a look of horror passed across his own face.

"What is it?" asked one of the Mrs. Peacocks.

"I just remembered something," he began timidly. "This isn't my intelligence-multiplying machine at all."

"It's not?" asked another one of the Peacocks. "What is it then?"

"It's my cloning machine."

"Your *cloning* machine?" asked a third Mrs. Peacock.

"Yes. It makes duplicates of anyone I aim the beam at. But there's no cause for alarm." The Professor scratched his head. "I just wish I could remember why I decided never to use this thing."

Five of the Mrs. Peacocks now began arming themselves with weapons. They moved slowly toward Plum and the real Mrs. Peacock.

"Ah, yes," said Plum. "Now I've got it. You see, there's a bug in the machine. The clones turn out to be identical to the original in every respect except one. They're crazed killers."

The real Mrs. Peacock screamed and ran from the room. "I wonder what got into her?" said Plum. Then he glanced at the clones, who were almost upon him. That jogged his memory. He screamed and ran from the room as well.

Meanwhile, in the Dining Room . . .

Meanwhile, in the Dining Room, Mr. Boddy was filling a cereal bowl with sugar. Then he added one cereal flake and poured in the milk. "Mmmm," he murmured happily as he began to eat.

"How about a little sugar with your cereal?" teased Mrs. Peacock as she entered the room. "Or should I say, how about a little cereal with your sugar?"

"I admit I like it sweet," said Boddy with a grin. "Do you want some?"

"Love some," said Mrs. Peacock, moving closer.

Just then, a second Mrs. Peacock appeared in the doorway.

"Mrs. Peacock," said Mr. Boddy. "What a coincidence. I was just talking to you."

Then his head swivelled rapidly back and forth between the two Mrs. Peacocks. Finally his head stopped. Because he now saw that the second Mrs. Peacock was holding a Revolver.

His head swivelled one more time. And he saw that the first Mrs. Peacock wasn't eating cereal.

87

Instead, she had taken out a Knife. She was only inches away.

"Stand back!" he yelled, "or I'll — " He looked down at the weapon in his hand. It was a spoon.

He ran screaming from the room with both Mrs. Peacocks racing right after him.

Mr. Boddy almost ran smack into Miss Scarlet, who was running the other way. There were two Mrs. Peacocks after *her*, as well.

Miss Scarlet sprinted into the Ball Room and slammed the door shut. A peacock feather was sticking through the crack in the door. It tickled Miss Scarlet's cheek as it slowly withdrew.

Then the clones started battering down the door.

Miss Scarlet began barricading the door with furniture.

When the door was secure, she looked around. The Ball Room had four doors. She ran from door to door, locking each one.

Except she didn't get to the fourth door in time.

It opened. And in walked Mrs. Peacock. She was gasping for breath.

"Don't be frightened," she said. "I'm the real Mrs. Peacock. And I'm in as much danger as you are. You see, Professor Plum — "

"I know, I know," said Miss Scarlet, swooning onto the love seat. "Lock the door."

But before Mrs. Peacock could lock the door, Miss Scarlet was on her feet again. "Wait a minute, how do I know you're the real Peacock? And not some dirty liar?"

"Don't say dirty," said Mrs. Peacock, horrified. "That's vulgar and rude."

Miss Scarlet sank back onto the love seat. "Whew! For a moment there, I didn't trust you."

Mrs. Peacock reached down to lock the door. But the door flew open before she could turn the latch.

A second Mrs. Peacock burst into the room. "She's lying," said this second Mrs. Peacock. "I'm the real one."

"So am I," said a third Mrs. Peacock, who had walked in behind her.

"Don't listen to them," said the first Mrs. Peacock, moving to Miss Scarlet's side.

"I won't," said Miss Scarlet. "I know you're the real one because — "

"I can't believe you would lie like that," interrupted the second Mrs. Peacock, staring at the first Mrs. Peacock. "That is so rude."

"You're lying, too," said the third Mrs. Peacock. "What horrible manners!"

"Uh oh," said Miss Scarlet. She said it for two reasons.

Reason #1: Since all three Mrs. Peacocks were prim and prissy, she no longer knew for sure who was telling the truth.

Reason #2: The first Mrs. Peacock had just placed the Rope around her neck.

Miss Scarlet slid down out of the loop of Rope. She also slid off the love seat. "You're *all* lying!" she screamed. She ran for the one open door.

All three clones ran after her. They all got to the door at the same time, which meant they crashed into each other and fell to the floor.

Meanwhile, another Mrs. Peacock was chasing Mr. Green and Colonel Mustard through the secret passageway from the Study to the Kitchen. Mrs. Peacock was gaining on them. Her hands stretched toward Mr. Green. She lunged.

But just then, Mr. Green saw that his shoelace was untied, and he bent down to tie it. Mrs. Peacock sailed over his head with a crash. Colonel Mustard tripped over her and was sent sprawling to the floor.

All three scrambled to their feet, Mrs. Peacock raised the Lead Pipe, bringing it down swiftly over Mr. Green's head.

But luckily for Mr. Green, he now saw that his other shoelace had come untied. He bent down to tie it. Thanks to his untied shoe, the blow missed by a foot.

Colonel Mustard and Mr. Green both screamed and ran through the passageway and into the Kitchen. The Peacock clone was in hot pursuit.

Meanwhile, Professor Plum and the other guests had gathered in the Conservatory. "You've got to do something," said Mr. Boddy as Professor Plum paced up and down.

"I am doing something," said the Professor. "I'm pacing."

"You must do something to stop these killer clones," explained Boddy.

"Ah," said Plum. "That's a little more difficult."

"We're doomed," said Mrs. White, nervously pulling on her hair.

"Don't say that!" cried Miss Scarlet, also pulling nervously on Mrs. White's hair.

"I don't think the situation is too serious," said Plum. "The worst that could happen is that the clones will kill us all."

Just then, the door opened and Mr. Green raced in. "Save me! Save me!" he yelled. Colonel Mustard ran in after him.

"That's odd," said Plum. "Why would Mr. Green be running from the Colonel?"

"You blockhead, he wasn't running from *me*," said Mustard. "He was running from — "

"From me," said Mrs. Peacock as she walked into the room.

"Or was it me?" said a second Mrs. Peacock.

"Or me."

"Or me."

"Or me."

The room was now crowded with Mrs. Peacocks.

"Six of them," said Plum in a quavering voice as the six Mrs. Peacocks all began to move slowly forward.

91

"There's got to be some way to reverse what you've done," said Mustard, slowly backing up.

"Reverse?" said Plum. "That's it!" He ran to his contraption and pointed it at the six Mrs. Peacocks. "Don't take another step! Or I'll press the reverse button. You'll be erased forever."

The six Mrs. Peacocks paused, eyeing him warily.

"What are you waiting for, Plum?" said Mr. Green.

"He's waiting because he doesn't know which of us to erase," said one Mrs. Peacock.

"There's no way to tell," said another.

"Plum, how do we tell?" asked Miss Scarlet.

Plum scratched his head. "Well, let's see. Which of these six Peacocks has a weapon?"

All six Peacocks held up both hands. Every hand was empty. They had all ditched their weapons.

Suddenly, Plum slapped his forehead. "I just remembered something!" he cried. "There are two bugs in my cloning machine, not one."

"Terrific," said Mrs. White without enthusiasm.

"The clones turn out to be crazed killers," continued Plum. "But they also have another flaw. The clones always lie."

"Thank goodness," said one of the Peacocks with a broad smile. "That proves I'm the real Peacock. I always tell the truth."

"That's a lie," insisted the other five.

"How does this help us?" asked Mrs. White.

"We just have to ask the right question," said Mr. Boddy. He thought for a moment. Then he asked, "Which one of you is real?"

"I am," answered all six.

"Which one of you always mind her manners?" asked Colonel Mustard.

"I do," answered all six again.

"State your name," ordered Mr. Green.

"Mrs. Peacock," answered all six Peacocks at once.

"I don't think this is getting anywhere," said Miss Scarlet.

"There's got to be a question we can ask that will tell us who's who," said Mr. Boddy.

"There isn't," said Mustard. "I'm afraid we'll just have to zap all of them!"

"Right," said Plum, aiming his machine.

"Wait!" cried Mrs. White. "I know what question to ask."

WHAT QUESTION SHOULD THE GUESTS ASK TO FIND THE REAL MRS. PEACOCK?

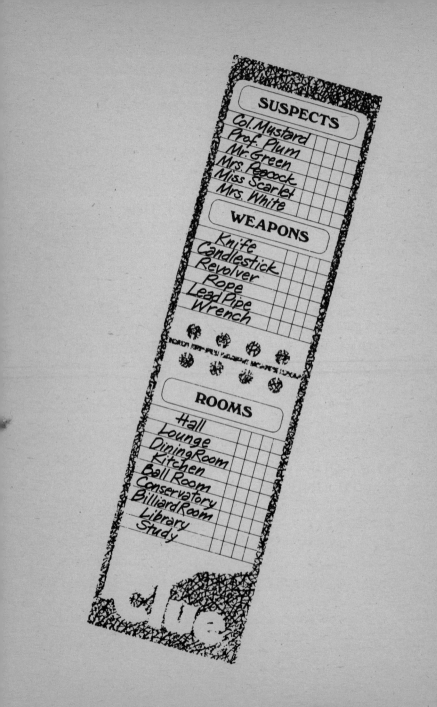

SOLUTION

"What's two plus two?" will work just fine, since only the real Mrs. Peacock will answer, "Four." The clones will all lie and make up some other answer. In fact, the guests can ask any simple factual question and solve the mystery.

10.
The Late Mr. Boddy

"**O**UR HOST IS LATE," SAID MR. GREEN, popping a dinner roll into his mouth and a silver fork into his pocket.

"You would think," said Colonel Mustard, "that Mr. Boddy would know better than to leave us all alone in the Dining Room — with his gold Candlesticks." He slipped both Candlesticks under his jacket.

"He trusts us, the dear man," said Professor Plum, who was busy stuffing some of Mr. Boddy's fine china into his briefcase.

"It's true," said Mrs. White with a laugh. "Mr. Boddy must be the most trusting man alive." She took off her white maid's cap. Underneath were stacked several packets of bills. "I cleaned out his safe," she explained. "And if he catches me, I'll just say I'm borrowing the money. He's so trusting, he'll believe me!"

"That's nothing," said Mrs. Peacock. "I'm sure I've taken more from Mr. Boddy than any of you. Each time I come here I leave with some priceless Boddy relic wrapped up in one of Mr. Boddy's fluffy towels. My fluffy towel collection alone is now worth thousands."

"And I've taken a million dollars worth of the old boy's artwork," boasted Plum.

"Child's play," said Colonel Mustard. "You read about yesterday's robbery at the Little Falls bank? I got two million in jewels from Mr. Boddy's safety-deposit box. Mr. Boddy called me on the phone afterward and asked me to help the police catch the thief!"

The guests laughed and applauded happily.

"Bravo," said Mr. Green. "But I can top that. I helped Mr. Boddy with his taxes this year. And secretly funnelled off three million into my own account."

"Peanuts," scoffed Miss Scarlet. "I conned Mr. Boddy into giving four million to a phony charity. I told him the money was for research into the dread disease, Missscarletosis, which turns its victims bright red." She was almost laughing too hard to speak. "I had him make the check out to Miss Scarlet!"

The guests were all laughing helplessly now as Miss Scarlet added, "He's the only one who would turn bright red — if he knew!"

"Miss Scarletosis," wheezed Mr. Green. He slapped the table. "That's too much!"

"Wait a minute!" said Plum suddenly. The guests quieted down and waited. "Mr. Boddy asked me to tell you something."

"What?" prodded Miss Scarlet.

Plum thought. "I haven't remembered that part yet."

"About the new intercom," said a crackly voice.

"Oh, right," said Professor Plum. "He asked me to tell you that he wants to test out a new intercom. And that he's upstairs right now listening to every word we say."

The guests looked at Plum in horror.

"You're joking," said Mrs. Peacock.

"Not at all," said the crackly voice.

The guests looked around frantically. "There!" said Mrs. White, pointing at the white intercom panel on the far wall.

Mr. Green ran to the panel. "I'm shocked!" he said into the intercom. "Shocked to hear what scoundrels the rest of you are!"

Colonel Mustard tried to push Green out of the way. "The rest of you were telling the truth?" he said into the intercom in a surprised voice. "I was making all that up!"

Mrs. White shoved her way to the intercom and said, "Mr. Boddy, I tricked them all into confessing so you could catch them. I deserve a promotion."

"You deserve something," said Mr. Boddy. "That's for sure."

He didn't say it through the intercom. He said it from the Dining Room doorway as he strode into the room.

"He *does* have Miss Scarletosis," said Plum, gazing at Boddy's red face.

"Shut up, you ninny," snapped Miss Scarlet. She smiled cattily at her host. "Reginald, darling, we were all kidding. We just wanted to show you that the intercom works."

"It works all right," said Mr. Boddy in a fury. "So you all think you can get away with what you've done? We'll see about that!"

"Let's settle this like gentlemen, Mr. Boddy," said Colonel Mustard. "You and Mrs. Peacock fight a duel."

Mr. Boddy ignored him. "All the years I've invited you to stay at my mansion. And this is my reward." He shook his head sadly. Then he turned and marched out of the room.

"Where are you going?" Mr. Green called.

"To call the police, of course," came the reply.

The guests all looked at one another in shocked silence.

"Now what?" said Mustard.

"Thrzonelloningoobuhdoo," said Professor Plum, who was calmly eating a peach.

"What?" asked Colonel Mustard.

Professor Plum swallowed. "Thrzonelloningoobuhdoo," he repeated.

"What are you trying to say?" asked Miss Scarlet, rolling her eyes.

"It's an ancient Sourdoo expression," explained

99

the Professor. "Loosely translated, it means, 'There's only one thing to do.' "

"And what's that?" Mrs. White asked him.

Everyone answered the question at once. "Kill Boddy."

"So? Are we all agreed?" Mrs. White asked.

"I don't *relish* the idea," said Mustard, "but there's no other way."

"Agreed," said Green.

"Right then," said Mustard, snapping into action. He handed out six Revolvers.

"Why do we all need Revolvers?" asked Mrs. Peacock. "Surely one of us could do the job?"

"This way we're all in it together," explained the Colonel. "And nobody can blackmail anybody."

He pulled out a box of bullets. "Aren't these nice?" he asked. "They come in six colors."

He started handing out the ammo. He gave the red bullets to Mrs. Peacock, the blue bullets to Mrs. White, the white bullets to Miss Scarlet, the purple bullets to Mr. Green, the yellow bullets to Professor Plum, and kept the green bullets for himself.

"I don't like this color," whined Miss Scarlet. She switched with Mrs. White, who had already switched her bullets with Professor Plum.

"Ready now?" said the Colonel. "Let's all load our Revolvers."

They loaded their weapons.

Mr. Green was scowling. "I don't like the feel of my weapon," he complained.

"I'll switch with you," said Miss Scarlet. She handed him her Revolver. And she took Mr. Green's.

"Are we all set *now*?" asked Mustard, his monocle twitching.

In response, Mrs. Peacock switched her Revolver with Miss Scarlet.

And Professor Plum switched with Mrs. Peacock.

Colonel Mustard fired his Revolver in the air. "Enough!" he shouted. "We have work to do."

In the locked library, Mr. Boddy trembled with rage as he dialed the police. At least he tried to dial the police. He was trembling so much that first he called a dry cleaners, then he called a zipper repair shop. Then he called a man named Bert. The next three times he got a busy signal.

As he dialed once again, he glanced nervously around the room. Both doors were locked. There was no way the guests could get in, he promised himself.

Finally, he got through to the police. "Yes, officer," Boddy began, "this is an emergency. Please send every available squad car at once to the following address. One — "

BANG! BANG! The shots rang out.

Mr. Boddy was right, there was no way the guests could get in. But their bullets travelled easily through the wooden doors. Boddy was hit with blue and red bullets.

"Hello?!" said the voice on the phone. "Hello?! Are you okay?"

The receiver fell to the floor with a clunk.

Mr. Boddy soon followed.

"Hello?" the policeman shouted.

But there would be no answer from Mr. Boddy, ever again.

WHO KILLED MR. BODDY?

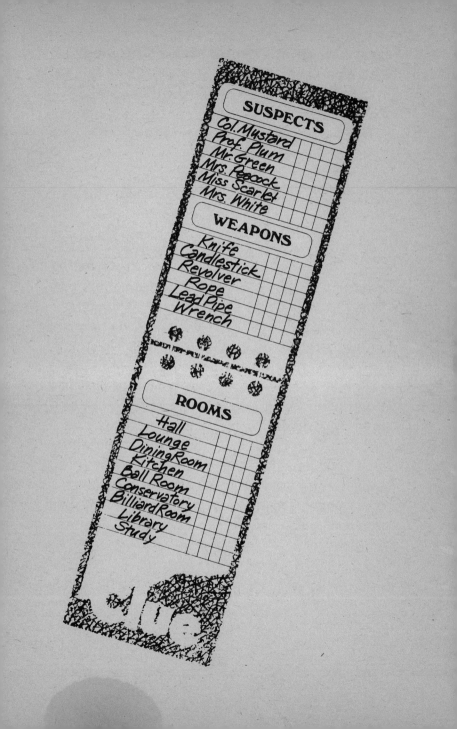

SUSPECTS

Col. Mustard				
Prof. Plum				
Mr. Green				
Mrs. Peacock				
Miss Scarlet				
Mrs. White				

WEAPONS

Knife				
Candlestick				
Revolver				
Rope				
Lead Pipe				
Wrench				

ROOMS

Hall				
Lounge				
Dining Room				
Kitchen				
Ball Room				
Conservatory				
Billiard Room				
Library				
Study				

SOLUTION

MISS SCARLET and MRS. PEACOCK with their REVOLVERS

First Plum switched with Mrs. White. So Plum had blue bullets, and Mrs. White had yellow ones.

Then Miss Scarlet switched with Mrs. White. So Miss Scarlet had yellow bullets, and Mrs. White had white ones.

Mr. Green switched loaded guns with Miss Scarlet. So Green had yellow bullets, and Miss Scarlet had purple ones.

Miss Scarlet switched with Mrs. Peacock. So Mrs. Peacock had purple bullets, and Miss Scarlet had *red* ones.

And finally, Mrs. Peacock switched with Plum. So Plum ended up with purple bullets, and Mrs. Peacock with *blue* bullets.